ASTRO CHIMP

SINCE THE 1940s,
HUMANS HAVE BLASTED
ANIMALS INTO SPACE.
MOST NEVER RETURNED.
THIS IS THE STORY OF
WHAT HAPPENED
NEXT.

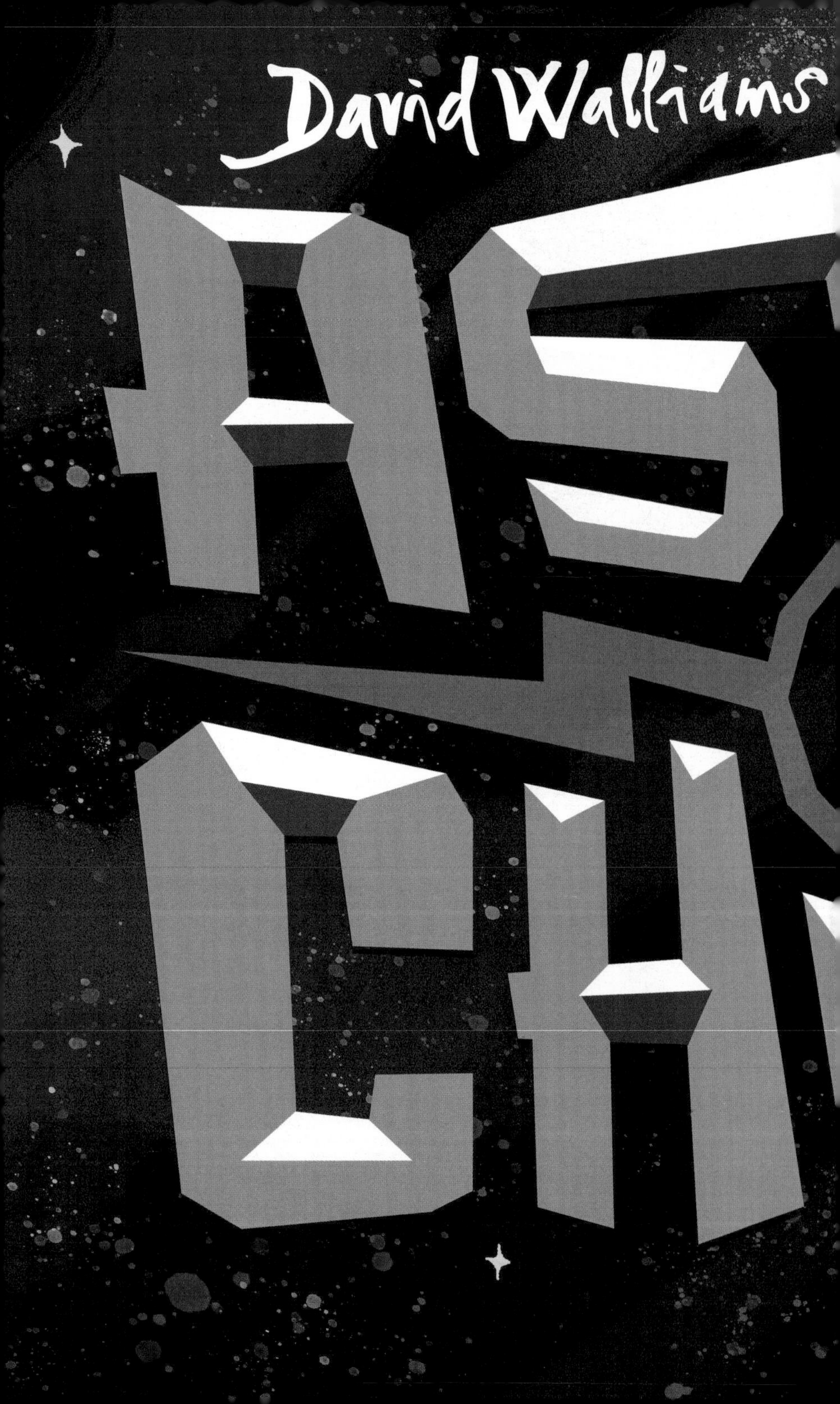
David Walliams

ILLUSTRATED
IN COLOUR BY
ADAM STOWER

HC
CB
HARPERCOLLINS
CHILDREN'S BOOKS

CHUMP
THE HERO

ALSO STARRING:

DMITRI
THE ROGUE

BARDOT
THE COOL CAT

THE
GIANT FRUIT FLIES
THE BADDIES

TING AND **HONG**
THE DO-GOODERS

CHOTI
THE
GERBIL
THE MYSTERY

EPISODE ONE

The rocket lifted off the ground, and shot into the sky like a rocket. Oh, it's already a rocket. All right, then, it shot off into the sky faster than something else that was still really, really, **really fast!**

The pale sky turned dark.
  Chump peered through the porthole.
  He was now so far away from Earth that he could see it was round.

The rocket boosters detached.

KERDUM!

WOO-HOO! I'M THE FIRST APE IN SPACE!

Small blasters on the underside of the capsule fired.

SHERRR!

The course was set.

The

capsule

began

orbiting

Earth.

Somewhere, thousands of miles below, was Chump's home, Central Park Zoo. He had arrived there as an orphan. The baby didn't have a name, so the other chimps named him Chump. That's because he was always amusing everyone by being silly.

One day, scientists from the US space agency, NASA, visited the zoo. They needed to choose a chimpanzee to **blast** into space.

All the other chimpanzees were smart enough to hide behind the trees, so the scientists chose Chump, who was showing off to them all with some **BOTTOM WAGGLING!**

Little did Chump know that he had been selected for a deadly-dangerous mission. NASA wanted to find out what happened when an ape orbited Earth. If it could survive, then chances were a human could too.

With Chump the chimp at the controls of a spacecraft, what could possibly go **wrong?**

As it turned out, *everything.*

Chump peeked through the porthole and waved.

HELLO, DOWN THERE! IT'S CHUMP! CAN YOU HEAR ME?

Of course they couldn't, but Chump didn't realise that. He wasn't the smartest.

But all the animals in the zoo were gazing up as the tiny dot disappeared into the black. The whole world was watching too.

Except a man called Colin, who was sitting on the loo and missed the whole thing.

HISTORY WAS BEING MADE!

The continents, the oceans and the polar icecaps drifted by, thousands of miles below.

Once he had spotted North America coming round again, Chump realised he had successfully orbited Earth.

On Chump's screen, all the NASA scientists down at Kennedy Space Center clapped and cheered.

"HOORAY!"

Chump cheered himself.

HOORAY FOR ME!

"Chump!" cried the chief scientist. "The mission is a success! Now sit tight as we bring you safely back to Earth!"

Chump kissed the camera,

leaving it drenched in dribble.

"Now, Chump," said the chief, "whatever you do, **DON'T PRESS THE RED BUTTON!"**

Still strapped into his seat, the chimp looked up. Above his head was a red button, just out of reach.

In big bold letters it read:

NEVER, EVER PRESS THIS BUTTON!

With the smuggest of smug looks on his hairy face, he took off the skin, and tossed the fruit part into the air.

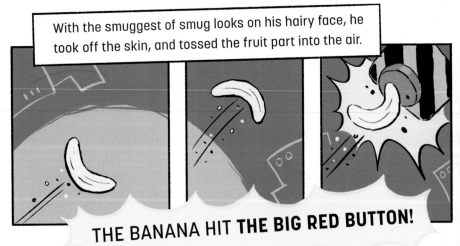

THE BANANA HIT **THE BIG RED BUTTON!**

Chump quickly put his helmet on as the ice-cold vacuum of space sucked all the warm air **out** of the capsule.

And – even worse than that –

THE BANANA SKIN too!

The capsule spun through the solar system...

past Mars, Jupiter, Saturn and Uranus...

before nearly colliding with Neptune.

Out there, space was two hundred times colder than ice.

The chimpanzee was frozen completely solid.

Like an ape lolly.

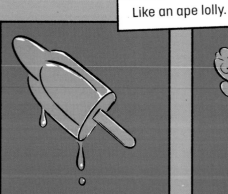 

Chump would remain frozen for the next **fifty years.**

That is

until he was

rudely awakened!

FIFTY
YEARS
LATER

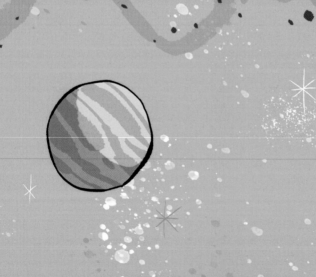

KERUNCH!

Metal struck metal!

Chump's capsule had been rammed by a **huge** spaceship. A pirate's skull-and-crossbones flag flew on top of it.

The ship locked on to the open emergency escape hatch of Chump's capsule.

Instantly, the ice-cold capsule was flooded with warm air.

The deep-frozen chimp* began to thaw.

Now Chump's ice-encrusted eyes opened for the first time in half a century!

An upside-down dog's head sporting an eyepatch poked through the hatch. The dog barked in a Russian accent.

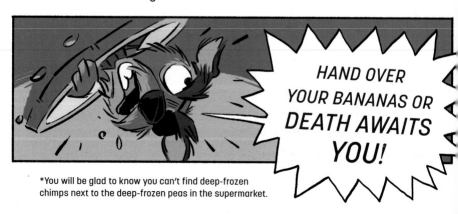

HAND OVER YOUR BANANAS OR DEATH AWAITS YOU!

*You will be glad to know you can't find deep-frozen chimps next to the deep-frozen peas in the supermarket.

Dmitri was a stray who had been found living rough on the mean backstreets of Moscow. Years before Chump's mission, he was selected to make history as the first animal in space.

The Russian space programme chose a stray dog, as it would be more able to endure the cold and hunger up in space.

Dmitri was strapped into his spacecraft and blasted up into space. His mission was a success: he survived!

But little did HE know that there was no plan to bring him back to Earth. He was left alone in his craft, floating across the universe. He had **ZERO CHANCE OF SURVIVAL.**

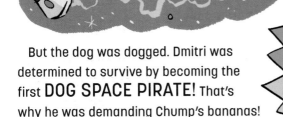

But the dog was dogged. Dmitri was determined to survive by becoming the first **DOG SPACE PIRATE!** That's why he was demanding Chump's bananas!

Feeling as if he were going to lose his bananas and his life, Chump searched for something to throw at the dog.

He reached into the tiny hatch marked **EMERGENCY BANANAS.**

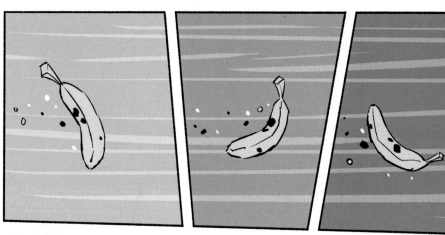

Hurling a frozen banana proved to be a MISTAKE. The dog caught it in his mouth and wolfed it down in one.

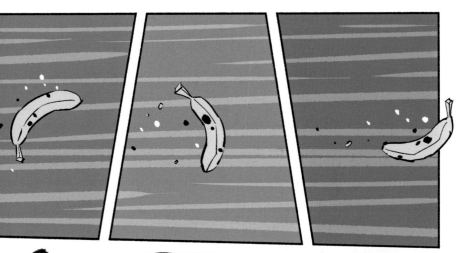

What does a space pirate do?

I attack and seize other spaceships, stealing their booty!

I'm rather attached to my booty.

I mean **booty** booty – anything and everything of value. Then I force the animals on board to walk the plank!

The chimp took off his still-snot-splattered helmet.

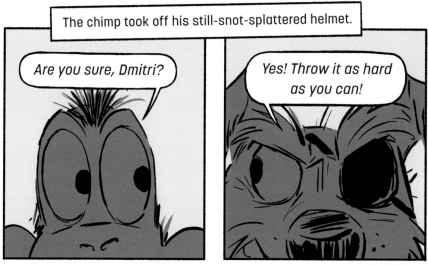

The helmet struck the screen, smashing it to pieces.

OOPS, I am SO sorry!

You wanna play, do you, banana boy?

No!

Well, let's play, then!

With that, Dmitri picked up the helmet and hurled it back.

WHIZZ!

THWUNT!

CLUNK!

You nearly hit me!

ODE
REE

Chump into his space-pirate ship. It was
size of Chump's. No wonder, as it had been
put together from lots of other spaceships. Dmitri had
joined them all to create one EPIC SHIP!

It was a **hodgepodge**,
but a mightily impressive **hodgepodge!**

The **Hound of Horror** is the mightiest ship in the known universe, made from all the ships I have plundered over the years. Yours is now just a tiny part of my giant craft.

Chump popped his hand in the air.

WHAT?

Can I say something?

If you must.

Thank you. Seeing as you have stolen my capsule, please can you give me a ride back home?

Home?

Yes, I need to get back to Earth.

Ha! You still call Earth home?

Dmitri put on his best pirate voice.

OTHER THINGS THAT DOG SPACE PIRATES DO:

Give their spaceships silly names.

Rip a few holes in their spacesuits to make it look as if they've been in a deadly swordfight.

Let their beards grow long. No trimming in the space-dog groomers, please! In fact, no grooming in the space-dog groomers at all!

Learn the fiddle so they can play and sing space shanties.

Eat and drink too much. Especially dog biscuits.

Wear an eyepatch, even if they can see perfectly well out of both eyes.

Wear two eyepatches. Not sensible.

Laugh heartily, even when things aren't that funny.

Wear three eyepatches. Just plain silly.

Attach a parrot space pirate to their shoulder.

Be a bit rude to people.

Nail a plank to their spaceship.

Dmitri ducked and the snot splattered all over a screen behind him.

"OOPS!" said Chump.

Dmitri looked at the chimp with disgust. "Revolting! Now, where were we?"

"You were about to make me walk the plank!" replied Chump, before slapping his hairy forehead in frustration.

Soon they were standing beside an airlock at the far side of his ship. Chump had to think fast if he was to live. However, thinking fast was not something he was good at.

"After you," growled Dmitri, politely murderous and murderously polite. Reluctantly, the chimp lolloped ahead.

Do you think there is any chance I might be rescued out there?

Dmitri chuckled. "We are at the furthest edge of the solar system. The nearest ship might be a million miles away."

Chump scratched his head. "Is that a long way away?"

"YES! A MILLION MILES!"

"How far is that?"

"A MILLION MILES IS A MILLION MILES!"

"All right! There's no need to shout!"

AIRLOCK

Dmitri huffed and put on his helmet, before pressing a button next to the airlock door.

It slid open.

SCHTUM!

Now there was just one outer door between them and COLD, DARK, ENDLESS SPACE.

Chump peered through the porthole.

ATISHOO!

He sneezed all over the glass.

OOPS!

Snot oozed down the porthole.

I AM NOT HAVING A SNOTTY SPACE-PIRATE SHIP! PEOPLE WILL TALK! NOW WIPE THAT OFF!

I don't have a tissue!

"HUH!" huffed Dmitri, whipping out a dirty hanky and pushing it into the chimp's hand.

"ATISHOO!" sneezed Chump, catching a huge globule of chimp snot in the hanky.

"LET ME DO IT!" thundered Dmitri, snatching it back. Instantly, he began wiping the glass, only making it worse by moving the snot around.

Chump began tiptoeing backwards until he was behind the inner door.

EPISODE
FOUR

A terrified Chump hit a button, and the inner door began to close.

SCHTU...!

But, before it shut completely, Dmitri smacked against it!

THWUMP!

He toppled backwards and hit the deck...

BOOF!

...trapping the end of his tail in the tiniest gap between the inner door and the floor.

YOWCHHH!

Chump wasn't good at left and right and by mistake pressed the button on his right. This opened the outer door.

74

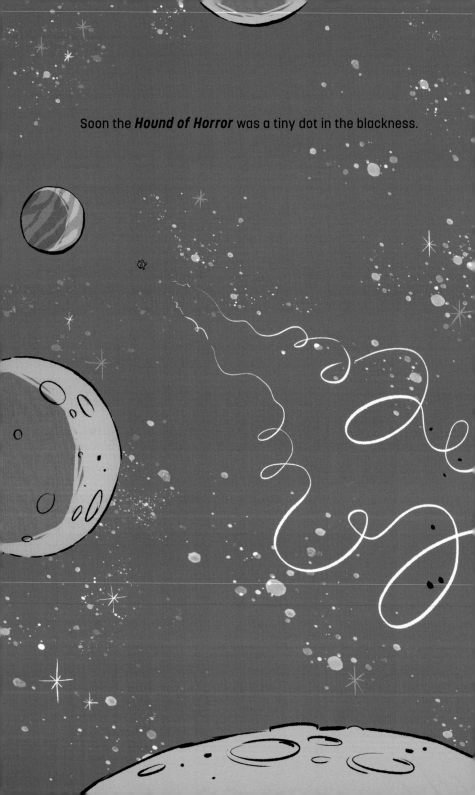

Soon the *Hound of Horror* was a tiny dot in the blackness.

The pair turned round to see A SWARM OF FRUIT FLIES buzzing towards them!

Only as the flies zoomed closer, did Chump realise how big they were – at least twice the size of him and Dmitri!

The giant flies dive-bombed the pair.

WHOOSH!

They grabbed hold of Chump and Dmitri and zoomed off!

ZOOM!

EPISODE FIVE

YES! A GIANT PINEAPPLE FLOATING IN SPACE!

Please be patient, as I will explain later how a giant pineapple came to be floating in space.

(And don't flick forward any pages – you will only spoil it for yourself.)

The spiky crown of the pineapple opened like a hatch, and the giant fruit flies flew in, clutching their prisoners.

Now Chump and Dmitri found themselves in a vast hollowed-out fruit.

To their surprise, the pineapple had been turned into a primitive spacecraft. There were levers, dials, a giant screen, keyboards, radios, even a **SELF-DESTRUCT** button! (These always seem like a bad idea.)

Everything looked as if it had been made from SPACE JUNK.

Dead satellites.

Unmanned rockets.

Space tools.

Parts that had fallen off space stations.

Random bits of machinery.

The swarm parted as an even taller fruit fly with bulging black eyes flew to the front. It was apparent this one was their leader. The one who must be obeyed! She hissed at them.

Fruit flies made news around the world as the very first living creatures to be sent into space. The fruit flies weren't given names, as there were too many of them. And they kept moving around.

Oh! Have we met before?

Oh yes! I am Queen Fruit Fly. And you stole our space rocket!

You've grown! How did you get so ginormous?

When you left us to die in space, Dmitri, me, my swarm and a pineapple were sucked into a black hole.

I hope it wasn't too dark in there! Ha! Ha!

But nobody was amused.

After a painful silence, Chump snorted. "I just got it! A black hole is dark because it's black! He's quite funny, isn't he?"

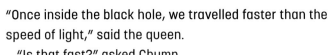

"Once inside the black hole, we travelled faster than the speed of light," said the queen.

"Is that fast?" asked Chump.

"Very. And please don't **interrupt!** It felt like we were in the black hole for all eternity and a millisecond all at once."

Both Chump and Dmitri looked puzzled.

"Around us was a kaleidoscope of colours and shapes. The mysterious forces at work in the black hole made our cells expand. We became **GIANT MEGA SUPER-INTELLIGENT ALL-POWERFUL WAR-MONGERING VILLAINOUS NOT-VERY-NICE MUTANT FRUIT FLIES!** The pineapple became a thousand times **bigger** too. Once we zoomed out of the end of the black hole, we found ourselves at the furthest edge of the galaxy. To survive, we took refuge in the giant pineapple. Over time, we ate out the inside and used debris we found floating in space to transform it into a spacecraft."

TEN EASY STEPS TO TURN A PINEAPPLE INTO A SPACESHIP

1. Find a friendly pineapple.

2. Locate a nice big black hole.

3. Hurl pineapple into black hole.

4. Wait at the other end for the giant pineapple to shoot out.

5. Hollow out the giant pineapple by eating the fruit. You could put chunks on a giant cocktail stick with some cheese, or place them in a blender to make a pineapple smoothie or bake a pineapple upside-down cake. All delicious. Unless you don't like pineapple.

6. Have a lie-down after eating all that pineapple.

7. Wake up.

8. Find bits of old space junk to furnish the interior.

9. Use pineapple juice as fuel.

10. Off you pop!

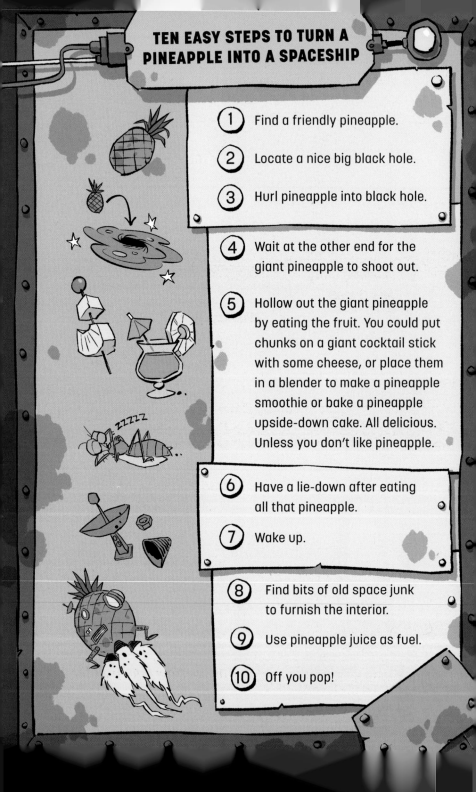

The swarm swarmed on the pair, their mouths open wide. All were hungry for **REVENGE!**

Chump and Dmitri, their faces contorted in *TERROR,* backed into each other.

Chump, being Chump, dashed the **wrong** way. . .
right towards the giant fruit flies!
  "WRONG WAY!" cried Dmitri.
  But it was too late! Chump was among them! He tripped
over one of the Queen Fruit Fly's feet and hit the deck!

THWONT!

Chump flew across the floor. . .
  SWOOFF!
  . . .knocking down fruit fly after fruit fly as he did!
  BOSH! BOSH! BOSH!

Amid all this commotion, the sly old dog snuck his way over to the controls of the craft.

Instantly, the pineapple twisted, soared and ducked like something that does all those things a fair bit.

All the insects and other animals were hurled around the pineapple.

They tumbled on top of each other! Before rolling round and round the pineapple!

ROMBLE! THWOMBLE! DROMBLE!

It was as if they were in a PINEAPPLE SPACESHIP TUMBLE DRYER!

The fruit flies tried to take off, but it was impossible. They all **BISH BASH BOSHED** into each other.

"NOW, MY ARMY OF FRUIT FLIES!" cried the queen. "DEVOUR THEM!" With that, she hurled Chump and Dmitri into the swarm.

PLEASE, MRS QUEEN!

Do you mind eating him first?

I SAID, "DEVOUR THEM!"

Our heroes were about to be EATEN ALIVE!

EPISODE
SIX

"EURGH!" exclaimed one of the fruit flies.

"THEY TASTE REVOLTING!"

Just the tiniest nibble of the dog or the chimp
was enough to make them all want to BARF!

The chimp and the dog shared a look and shrugged.
She was right. They **were** animals.

First, us fruit flies with all our fury will take our revenge on you two...

Why me, Mrs Queen? I haven't done anything to you!

...for our thousand fellow fruit flies that you ate!

But they tasted so deliciously of armpit!

The fruit flies were **furious.**

"HOW DARE YOU!" thundered the queen.

"Oops!" said Chump.

"You chump!" barked Dmitri.

"I know."

We will savour every moment of killing you! We love killing! Fruit mainly, but we are branching out. Chimps. Dogs. Whatever! And when we have killed you two until you are dead, we will wreak our revenge on the entire human race!

Why?

The queen looked around at her swarm.

We fruit flies made history as the first living creatures in space!

Oh, here we go again.

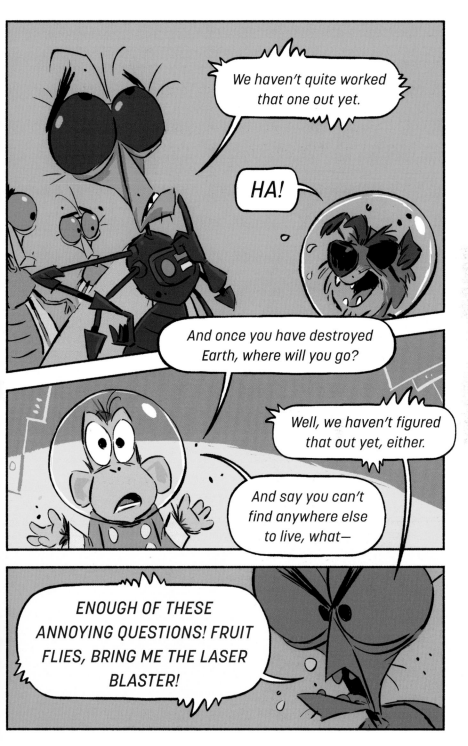

A huge homemade weapon was fetched from behind a glass case. It took the strength of four giant fruit flies to carry it. They handed it to the queen, who lifted it with ease and pointed it towards the pair.

Dmitri took a step
behind Chump,

who took a step
behind him,

who took a step
behind him,

who took a step
behind him.

This went on for a while.

It was the laser blaster itself that was zapped!
"ARGH!" cried the queen as the blaster dropped out of her front legs.

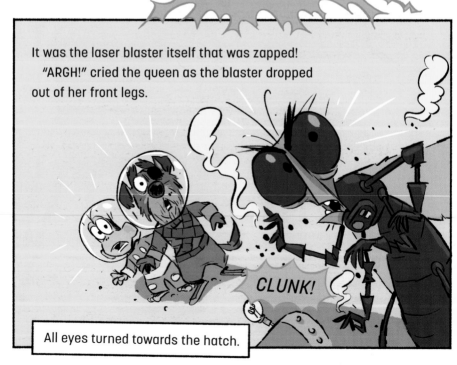

All eyes turned towards the hatch.

There was a cat with a jetpack strapped to her back!

The French space agency had selected this super-smart sassy cat to be their first animal in space.

The cat became an instant star, **THE WORLD'S FIRST CATSTRONAUT!**

But Bardot's space flight went dramatically wrong.

The world watched in horror as her rocket lost power. She became trapped thousands of miles above Earth.

There was a state funeral in Paris, with a cat-sized coffin – white, like her fur.

But the coffin was empty, as Bardot's body was never recovered.

Cats are said to have nine lives, and Bardot was determined her lives weren't over yet.

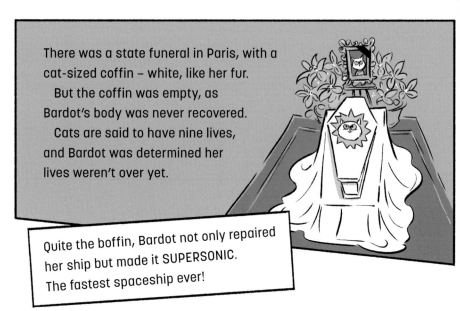

Quite the boffin, Bardot not only repaired her ship but made it SUPERSONIC. The fastest spaceship ever!

Bardot's plan was to police the universe: fight evil and be a force for good.

But it didn't quite work out that way, because she had the misfortune of meeting a certain dog space pirate.

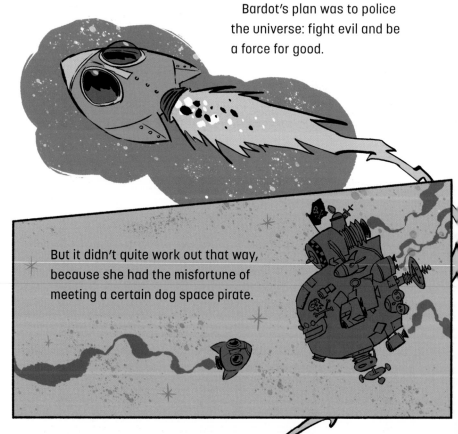

119

In half a second, Bardot **blasted** him.

ZAP!

Anyone else care to resist?

It will come as no surprise to learn that the pineapple fell deathly silent.

Nine of me, for my nine lives!
Why did you clone yourself?
There is so much wickedness in this universe. . .
Oh! Don't get me started on that!
You are one of the wicked ones, Dmitri!
Oh yes.

"Prisoners! Follow me!"

With that, Bardot marched Dmitri and Chump in the direction of the hatch.

Chump couldn't bear it.

He covered his eyes with his hands.

Then he covered his ears with his feet.

ZAP!

ZAP!

ZAP!

Bardot spoke into the microphone in her helmet.

BARDOTS! I NEED BACK-UP!

ZAP!

In an instant, the spiky end of the pineapple was hit by LASER BLASTS!

ZAP!

ZAP!

Then the pineapple began to **rumble.**

That rumble became a **wobble.**

That **wobble** became a **shake.**

And then the pineapple began to **crumble!**

The fighting stopped. Everyone fell silent.
They looked out of the porthole.

Something was hurtling through **space**!
Something bigger than a **meteorite**!
Something as big as the **moon**!
Something as big as a **planet**!
It was a **giant** brown-and-white globe!

AND IT WAS HEADING STRAIGHT FOR
THE PINEAPPLE!

So hard that all went silent. All went dark. All went WEIRD!
The chimp, the dog, the cats and all the fruit flies turned to jelly.

The pineapple ship was now hurtling through space at the speed of light.

It was only when it hit an asteroid field that it began to slow down.

The asteroids struck the spacecraft hard.

As the asteroids passed, the pineapple lurched to a halt, lost in the vast emptiness of space.

The radio crackled, and a croaky voice came on.

DO NOT FEAR! THE SPACE EMERGENCY RESCUE TEAM IS ON ITS WAY!

Space emergency rescue team?

By the time they get here, the emergency will be well and truly over!

Why? Who are they?

Tortoises!

The slowest creatures on Earth had become the fastest when they were fired into space from a Chinese space centre.

Once they'd found themselves abandoned up there, Ting and Hong were determined to help others in distress. So they turned their rocket ship into a rescue ship.

THE SPACE EMERGENCY RESCUE TEAM was born.

Of course, if you require rescuing, it needs to be fast.

Sadly, these tortoises didn't do fast.

They were the slowest rescue team in the universe!

"LOOK!" exclaimed the queen, pointing out of the porthole.

In the distance, a creaky old space rocket was idling along. **THE SPACE EMERGENCY RESCUE TEAM** was emblazoned on the side. But they had run out of space, so the "M" was missing. It read:

THE SPACE EMERGENCY RESCUE TEA

Providing cups of tea in emergencies didn't have the same sense of drama. Even if they came with biscuits.

All those aboard the pineapple shifted around awkwardly as they waited and **waited** and **waited.**

The silence was broken by what sounded like **THUNDER!**

Eventually, the rocket ship reached the pineapple. Not putting the brakes on in time, it pranged into the ship.

147

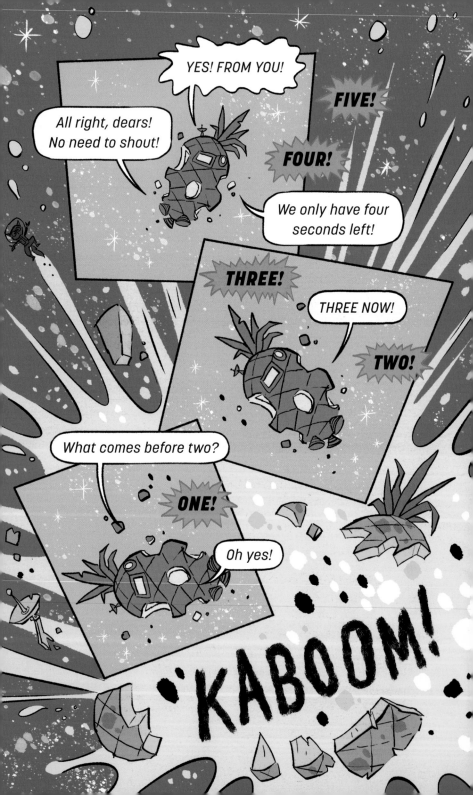

EPISODE
EIGHT

The pineapple blasted into a billion chunks!

Any surviving cat clones or fruit flies were hurled into the infinite.

A spinning Chump hit the tortoises' rocket.

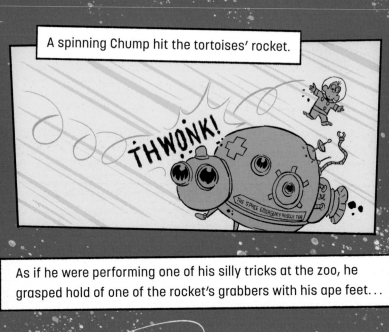

As if he were performing one of his silly tricks at the zoo, he grasped hold of one of the rocket's grabbers with his ape feet...

Dmitri grabbed on to Chump, Bardot grabbed on to Dmitri, Ting grabbed on to Bardot, Hong grabbed on to Ting and, ANNOYINGLY FOR EVERYONE EXCEPT HER, the queen grabbed on to Hong.

Chump swung with his feet, and they performed a loop-the-loop, ending up in a jumble inside.

THOMP!

The tortoises' tiny rocket was now full to bursting.
Tails tickled toes.
Whiskers itched tummies.
And noses were perilously close to bottoms.

THE SPACE EMERGENCY RESCUE

She yanked a lever, and the spacecraft lurched off at the speed of a sloth.

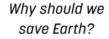

Why should we save Earth?

For a billion reasons!

Name one!

Earth is a beautiful planet, home to millions of forms of life. If we don't save it, they will be gone forever!

Chimps like me would be destroyed too!

I haven't got beef with the animals, it's the humans I despise. They left me up here to die!

"That's one way of looking at it," replied Bardot. "Another is that they took you off the streets, sent you on an adventure beyond your wildest dreams and made you the most famous dog of all time!"

DMITRI
SPACE
HERO

There is even a statue of you in Moscow!

THERE IS?

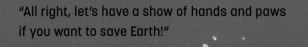

"All right, let's have a show of hands and paws if you want to save Earth!"

There were lots of straining noises as the creatures tried their best to raise their limbs in the crush.

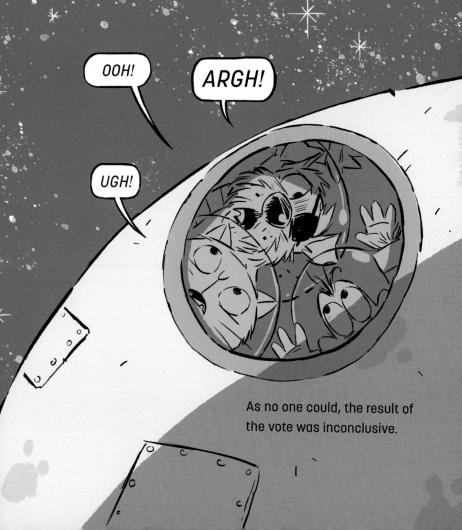

As no one could, the result of the vote was inconclusive.

Heads were shaken, eyes were rolled and sighs were sighed.

Bardot weaved past everyone and out of the rocket. Dmitri and Chump followed, and all three took a spacewalk. They went round to the back of the ship to soup up the engine. But nothing could have prepared them for what they found...

"THIS IS AN ATOMIC REACTOR!" exclaimed Bardot.

"Like an atomic bomb?" asked Dmitri.

"Exactly!"

"That must be why they chose tortoises for this mission. They had a greater chance of surviving the radiation. . ."

"Well, they have got shells," said Chump.

"It's because they're reptiles, Chump. Reptiles were the only creatures who survived the atomic bomb tests in the desert a century ago."

"If it's powered by an atomic reactor, why does this ship go so slowly?" asked Dmitri.

"That's what we've got to find out, boys!" said Bardot.

Soon Bardot, with the help of Dmitri, and no help from Chump, had repaired the spacecraft's atomic reactor.

The cat was sure this would now be THE FASTEST SHIP IN THE UNIVERSE! Even faster than hers, and hers was SUPERSONIC!

ALL RIGHT, TORTOISES! FIRE HER UP!

ROGER!

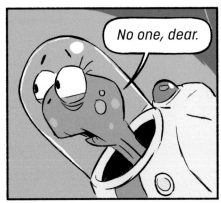

The spaceship zoomed off
at the speed of lightning.

Whatever Bardot had done, it had worked like a **DREAM!**

Sadly, that dream was about to
become a **NIGHTMARE!**

EPISODE
NINE

Our three heroes had been left standing. Well, floating.
THE SPACE EMERGENCY RESCUE TEAM had left them high and
dry. The spaceship was now just a dot, as far away as the
stars, while Chump, Bardot and Dmitri hung suspended,
helplessly, in space. The tortoises had done the
exact opposite of rescuing them. They
had ABANDONED them!

"LOOK! You can still just make out the asteroid field we passed through, which destroyed the pineapple," said Bardot, pointing off into the distance. "If you both hold on tight, I can use my jetpack to shoot us into its path. Come on, boys!"

WHOOSH!

The trick was to get just ahead of the asteroid field. That way, Chump, Dmitri and Bardot could leap on to an asteroid, or two, or three. That was their only chance of catching up with the rocket. And, of course, averting a long and lingering death, drifting in the endless emptiness of space.

Which wouldn't be nice.

In moments, they had zoomed into place, waiting for the storm to catch up with them.

As the asteroids were just about to strike, Bardot shouted, **"NOW!"**

Each of them leaped on to an asteroid!

The three of them had got the hang of it.

ASTEROID SURFING!

It might be THE MOST DANGEROUS SPORT IN THE GALAXY,* but right now it was the only chance our trio had of survival!

* THE MOST DANGEROUS SPORTS IN THE GALAXY ARE:
5. Arm wrestling with aliens. Some have hundreds of arms.
4. Planet football. Never a good idea trying to kick a planet. You might break your toe.
3. Swimming on Neptune. Far too cold. Bits snap off.
2. Cycling on the sun. Too hot. Tyres melt. Bikes melt. You melt.
1. Asteroid surfing.

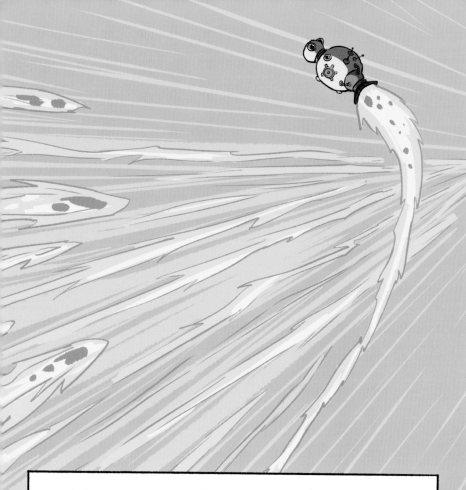

As they drew near, the rocket turned round. Now it was heading into the storm!

"I don't believe it!" said Bardot. "THE RESCUE SHIP IS ACTUALLY GOING TO RESCUE US!"

"YES!" said Chump, jumping for joy, and very nearly falling off his asteroid.

Now **A DARING STUNT** was required: leaping off the asteroids and landing on the rocket.

No easy task, going at this speed.

"WAIT FOR IT! WAIT FOR IT!" teased Bardot. **"NOW!"**

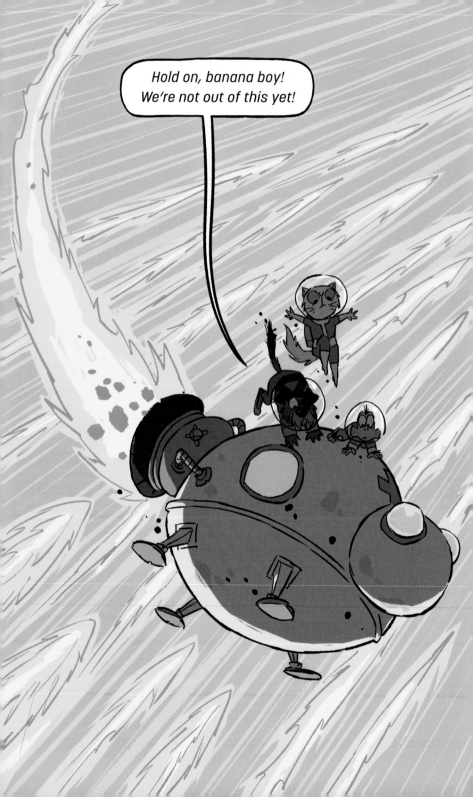

To avoid being destroyed by the asteroid shower (which is bad, but not as bad as an asteroid bath), the rescue ship made a dramatic turn.

WHOOSH!

Clinging on for dear life, the three animals were whisked out of the way, and zoomed off in the direction of Earth.

EPISODE
TEN

The atomic rocket, with our heroes now safely back inside, went at **atomic speed.**

ZOOOO

Far ahead, THE MYSTERIOUS GLOBE OF DOOM came into view, all the time looking bigger and bigger as the rocket drew nearer and nearer.

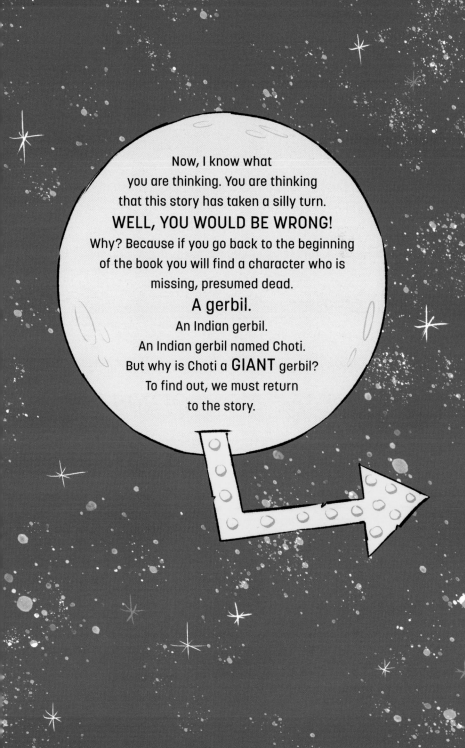

Now, I know what
you are thinking. You are thinking
that this story has taken a silly turn.
WELL, YOU WOULD BE WRONG!
Why? Because if you go back to the beginning
of the book you will find a character who is
missing, presumed dead.
A gerbil.
An Indian gerbil.
An Indian gerbil named Choti.
But why is Choti a **GIANT** gerbil?
To find out, we must return
to the story.

"That gerbil must have suffered the same fate as us fruit flies!" said the queen.

"A BLACK HOLE!" said Bardot.

"YES!"

"Why is she rolled up into a ball?" asked Dmitri.

"Lots of animals at the zoo would roll themselves into a ball when they were frightened," replied Chump.

"We tortoises disappear into our shells," said Hong.

"Of course!" exclaimed Bardot. "Hurtling through that black hole must have terrified this creature!"

"And being shot out the other end," agreed Chump.

Unfortunately for the giant gerbil, the humans felt differently. ALL AT ONCE, A HUNDRED MISSILES WERE LAUNCHED FROM EARTH RIGHT AT HER!

SPACE WAS

ABLAZE WITH
EXPLOSIONS!

The missiles exploded all around the giant gerbil, narrowly missing the rocket.

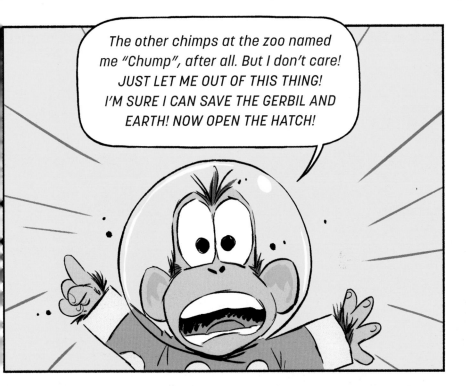

With that, our three heroes leaped out of the rocket and on to the giant gerbil!

Now they were GIANT-GERBIL SURFING!*

*DO NOT TRY THIS AT HOME. OR IN SPACE. IT IS EVEN MORE DANGEROUS THAN ASTEROID SURFING!

"Poor gerbil!" exclaimed Chump. "She must be terrified!"

"Any moment now, she is going to be blasted into a billion pieces," said Bardot.

"Taking us with her!" added Dmitri. "So, what are we going to do?"

"We need to steer her off her collision course with Earth," replied Bardot.

"But how? Gerbils don't have steering wheels!"

"No! But they do have tails," said Chump. "If I can find her tail, we might be able to yank her off course!"

BOOM! BOOM! BOOM!

The explosions blasted our heroes off their feet, but still they surged forward, on their hunt for the creature's tail.

The giant gerbil was now dangerously close to Earth.

Only when Chump tripped over something, did he realise what it was!

*OVER HERE!
I'VE FOUND HER TAIL!*

The chimp was right. That fluffy thing as thick as a tree trunk was indeed Choti's tail!

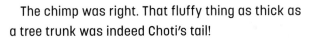

BOOM! BOOM! **BOOM!**

Using all their strength, the chimp, the dog and the cat lifted it. Bardot gave a signal to the tortoises. Ting and Hong lowered their rocket until it was hovering over the tip of the tail. Then, with the rocket's metal grabbers, they reached out to grasp it.

Just as it was within reach, the craft took a HUGE HIT!

KERANK!

Making sure Bardot was watching, Dmitri took a heroic leap at the queen. But the queen had mighty strength!

An EPIC BATTLE commenced!

Chump and Bardot tried to save him, but the queen thwacked them away.

THWOCK!

THWUCK!

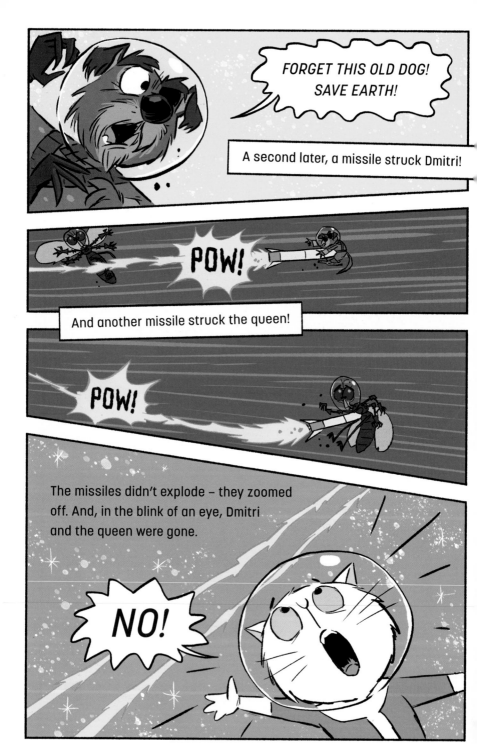

A tearful Chump cried, "WE HAVE TO DO THIS! NOW!"
He and Bardot lifted the end of the giant gerbil's tail.

The grabbers grabbed hold of it.

"AAARRRGHHH!" cried Choti. The pain made her uncurl in an instant!

A giant gerbil-shaped shadow plunged Earth into darkness.

Chump and Bardot leaped back into the spacecraft.
Impact with the planet was imminent.

BOOM! BOOM! BOOM!

As he was still closing the hatch, Chump shouted, "NOW!"
"What, dear?" asked Hong.
"Now, dear!" replied Ting.
"No need to shout, dear!"

Hong pulled a lever and the atomic engine exploded into life. The craft shot off, jerking the gerbil halfway across the solar system in a split second.

WHOOSH!

Now, Choti had no idea she was being rescued.

She thought she was being ATTACKED!

Let's not forget, her tail had been yanked. Hard.

Never upset a gerbil. Especially not a giant one. Gerbils may be cute and fluffy, but they BITE!

As she was dragged through space by her tail, Choti arched her back and went in for the kill.

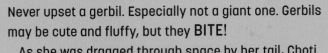

CHOMP!

"IT'S THE END!" cried Bardot.
The gerbil's giant razor-sharp teeth bit the rocket in two!

"ARGHHH!" they cried, spinning into space.

But who should come to the rescue, sitting astride a missile?
Dmitri! Flying the missile like a winged horse, controlling its
every twist and turn.

> *DO NOT FEAR! DMITRI*
> *IS HERE!*

"How are you working that thing?" asked Bardot.
"Easy! I found this spanner!" said Dmitri, holding up the
one Chump had dropped in space. "You will be glad to know
the queen was shot across the solar system by a missile,
which exploded on Pluto. She must have been blown into
a billion bits! Now hop on."

Chump looked over to see Choti whirling further and further into space. Soon this ginormous creature would be nothing but a speck in the infinite blackness.

The gerbil was sucked into a black hole that made her a million times bigger. I am sure there is a way to make her a million times smaller... to get her back to normal size.

I think I know where Chump is going with this!

How are we going to do that?

A BLACK HOLE!

EPISODE
TWELVE

THIS WAS THE DEADLIEST MISSION OF ALL!
TO SEND A GIANT GERBIL BACK UP
A BLACK HOLE!

ONE! The gang took Choti by surprise and grabbed hold of her tail.

TWO! They tied the end of her tail to the missile.

THREE! Dmitri powered the missile through space.

FOUR! They found the end of a black hole.

FIVE! They leaped off the missile just in time.

SIX! The missile pulled Choti into the black hole.

SEVEN! The gang all held on to Bardot, who powered them through space.

EIGHT! They reached the mouth of the black hole, keeping a safe distance so they would not be sucked in themselves.

NINE! They waited. And waited some more.

TEN! A minuscule missile shot out, towing a little gerbil.

The gang zoomed over to catch hold of the gerbil and untied her tail from the missile.

"EEK?" squeaked little Choti.

"I speak Gerbil!" replied Bardot. "EEK! EEEK! EEEEK! EEK!"

"EEK!" agreed Choti.

"What did you tell her?" asked Dmitri.

"The whole story! Now, Chump, you keep Choti safe!"

The chimp cradled the gerbil in his hand, and placed her inside his spacesuit.

"Where to now?" asked Bardot.

"Let's find my ship!" said Dmitri.

"Our ships!"

"Sorry. Our ships!"

They zoomed off into space in search of the **Hound of Horror**. Just as Bardot's jetpack was about to run out of power. . .

THERE!

A little while later, all the animals were safely on board.

"Now, it's time to break up the *Hound of Horror,* and give these spaceships back to their rightful owners," said Bardot.

Dmitri winced at the idea.

"Come on! Don't forget you're a good boy now!" said Bardot.

"HUH!" Dmitri huffed and went to work.

"WOW!" exclaimed Champ. "Thank you!"

"You don't have to thank me," replied Bardot. "We all must thank you, Champ, for saving Earth!"

With that, all the other creatures gave Champ a cheer.

"Together we could be a space force," said Champ. "THE ANIMAL SPACE FORCE! Saving not just Earth, but the entire universe!"

"YES!"

"So, where to, Captain Champ?" asked Bardot.

"Captain?" spluttered Champ.

"How come he's the captain and I'm not?" barked Dmitri.

"Be a good boy! Now, where to, Captain Champ?"

"Hmm. How about once round the universe?"

"AYE, AYE, CAPTAIN!" replied the others. Captain Champ counted them down.

FIVE!

FOUR!

THREE!

TWO!

ONE!

BLAST OFF!

EPILOGUE

Meanwhile, on Pluto, a creature was climbing out of the ice. A bruised, battered and burned creature. "REVENGE!" the queen fruit fly cried.

REV

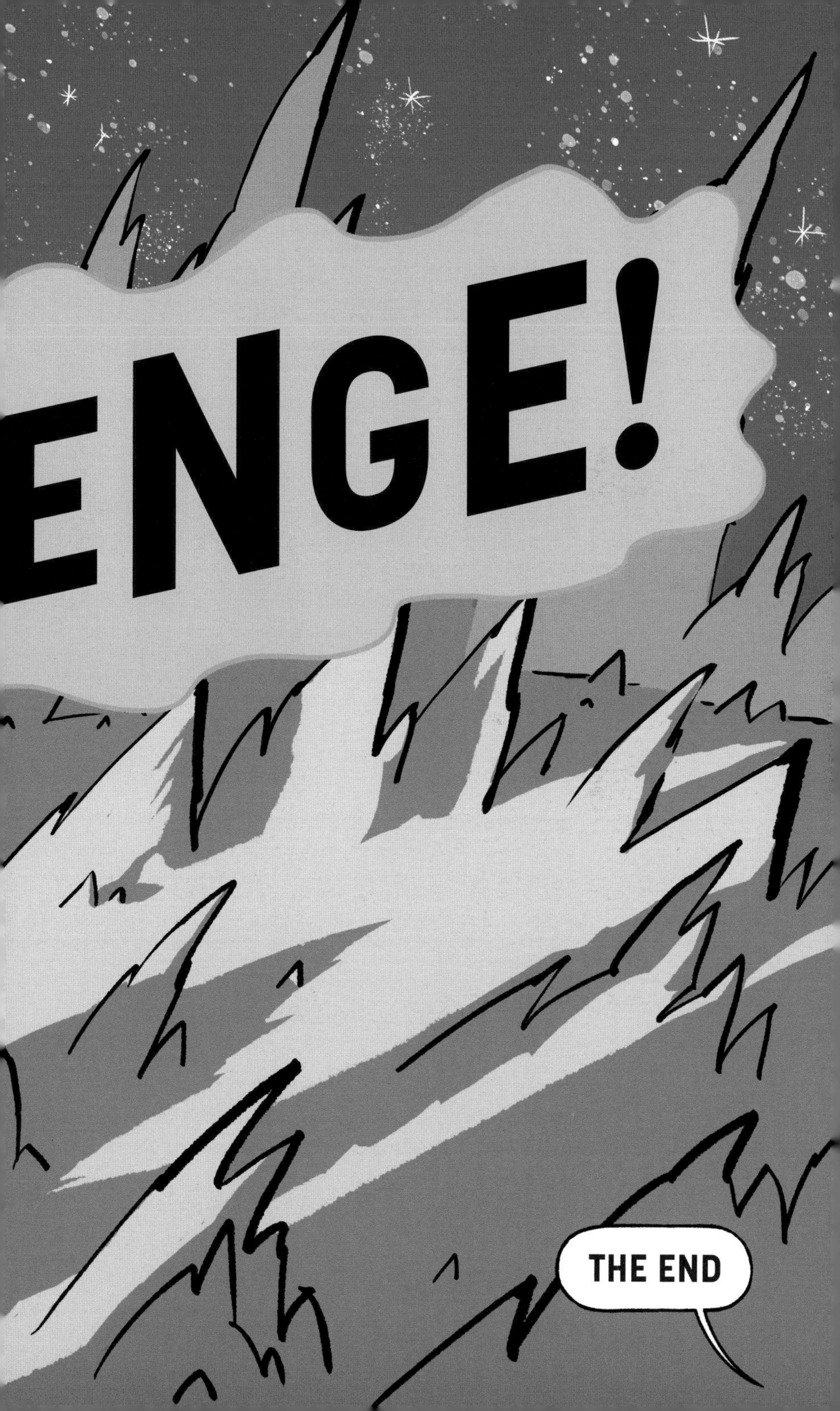
ENGE!
THE END

All the characters in **Astrochimp** are based o

 Fruit flies were indeed the first creatures to be sent into space, in 1947. It was a US mission, on a V-2 rocket. At that time, no one knew if any animal could survive in space. These fruit flies proved they could.

 Then, in 1949, there followed a rhesus macaque **monkey,** named Albert II. Again, this was a US mission using a V-2 rocket. Albert II was the first animal in space, if you don't count the fruit flies. Sadly, he died when the rocket's parachute failed to open on his return to Earth.

 The Russians were not to be outdone by the US. In 1957, they sent a stray **dog** named Laika on *Sputnik 2* to orbit Earth. She did not survive, but is still famous around the world. In Russia, there is a statue of the heroic Laika, and she is even commemorated on stamps and boxes of matches.

 As the space race heated up between these two competing nations, the US responded in 1959 by sending a rhesus macaque **monkey** named Miss Able and a squirrel monkey named Miss Baker into space on a Jupiter rocket. They made history by becoming the first monkeys to safely return to Earth.

 Chump was inspired by Ham the **chimpanzee.** In 1961 he became the first great ape in space. Ham was even given some responsibility in piloting his Mercury spacecraft. He returned safely to Earth and became a national hero.

NIMALS IN SPACE

e real animals that were blasted into space.

 France really did send a **cat** into space. In 1963, Félicette was sent up in a Veronique rocket. She survived her flight and has been honoured with a bronze statue in France, so she will never be forgotten.

 Argentina joined the space race in 1967 by launching a **rat** named Belisario into space on a Yarará rocket.

 Russia sent up two **tortoises** on *Zond 5* in 1968. They became the first animals to be blasted into deep space and circle the moon.

 Cross **spiders** named Anita and Arabella followed, joining astronauts on the US rocket *Skylab 3* in 1973.

 And in case you were thinking that **gerbils** were never blasted into space, they were! Russia sent them up in 2007! Their mission was to see if humans could survive a trip to Mars. One day, we might even see gerbils living on Mars.

Actually, that's a cool idea for a story. . .

First published in the United Kingdom by
HarperCollins *Children's Books* in 2024
HarperCollins *Children's Books* is a division of HarperCollins*Publishers* Ltd
1 London Bridge Street
London SE1 9GF

www.harpercollins.co.uk

HarperCollins*Publishers*
Macken House, 39/40 Mayor Street Upper
Dublin 1, D01 C9W8, Ireland

1

HB ISBN 978-0-00-858757-4
TPB ISBN 978-0-00-864955-5
PB ISBN 978-0-00-864957-9

A CIP catalogue record for this title is available from the British Library.
Printed and bound in Italy by Rotolito

MIX
Paper | Supporting
responsible forestry
FSC™ C007454

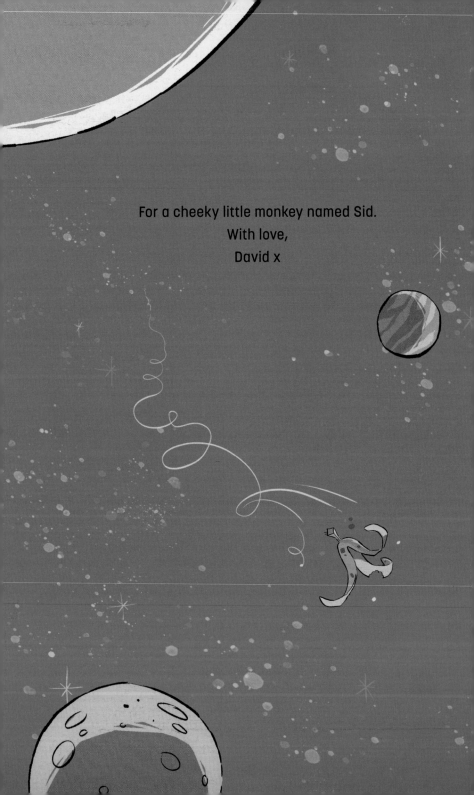

For a cheeky little monkey named Sid.
With love,
David x

DAVID WALLIAMS is a literary phenomenon. His books have been translated into fifty-five languages and have sold more than fifty-six million copies worldwide. They have achieved unprecedented critical acclaim and have spent a record-breaking 240 weeks at number one in the Children's charts.

ADAM STOWER is an award-winning author and illustrator. He has collaborated with David Walliams on several of his books for children, including *Spaceboy*, *Robodog* and *The World's Worst Monsters*.